The Adventures Of The Sea Rabbits Of Greystones

By Pip Carr

THE SEA RABBITS OF GREYSTONES

Copyright © 2016 Pip Carr
All rights reserved.
ISBN: 9781519032041

Flintlock Books
www.flintlockbooks.com

THE SEA RABBITS OF GREYSTONES

For my wonderful "Boys" Ollie and Max

THE SEA RABBITS OF GREYSTONES

CONTENTS

1	The meeting	Page 1
2	A surprise for Max	Page 9
3	A secret from the Sea	Page 13
4	The nine surprises	Page 17
5	Birthday party	Page 21
6	A new game for Max	Page 27
7	Lottie	Page 31
8	Two lost ducklings	Page 36
9	Sea Rabbit Treasure	Page 40
10	The Clickers	Page 45
11	A New a friend for Max	Page 49
12	Granny	Page 53

THE SEA RABBITS OF GREYSTONES

ACKNOWLEDGMENTS

With thanks to Maks and Andy for their illustrations and to my uncredited editor mainly for the cups of tea.

Special thanks to my friends and family who have been so encouraging

Thanks to my mum who I miss every day…

Thanks to Max for being my inspiration and my best friend.

THE SEA RABBITS OF GREYSTONES

1. THE MEETING

The sea rabbits lived in a cove on the North beach, by the pretty seaside village of Greystones. Their burrows were just above sea level, which they slept in during the night, but mainly they swam under the sea, a lot like seals.

They had lived there for many hundreds of years as it was a very safe place. The sea was never too rough to damage their burrows, which were made with a great deal of care so they never collapsed and the fishermen never bothered them, as it was too near to the coast for the trawlers. There were lots of fish in the cove which was also home to the seals. The rabbits like to play with the seals and they became great friends, often chasing each other in the sea.

The sea rabbits liked to eat seaweed, sugar kelp, and sea oak, all of which were in great supply, so they never went hungry.

One day when the sun was trying its best to peep from behind the clouds and the wind wasn't too gusty. Molly was taking her dog Max for a walk along the North beach. She liked to walk all the way down to the very end and sit on the old sea wall just to see the sea and watch the seagulls fly. Max liked to run into the water and try to catch the waves, which always made Molly laugh as Max would look at her as if to say "aren't I clever, do you want to play too?"

Molly was 10 years old and lived in Greystones village in a house not far from the sea, with her Granny, her parents and of course her dog Max. She loved to get up early and walk along the beach with Max, when nobody else was about.

Molly noticed whilst looking out across the horizon, several dark heads bobbing up and down in the sea. She thought they were seals as she had seen them swimming a couple of times, but this time the colour of the heads was a lot lighter and they seemed to have long sticky up ears!

She peered as hard as she could but couldn't make out whether they were seals or something else!

All of a sudden she heard an "oow oow oowwing" noise from somewhere near the wall. She jumped down from where she was sitting and began to follow the noise. To her surprise there was what looked like a baby seal, hidden near some rocks and it was calling for its mother, but looking again Molly noticed that it wasn't a seal but a rabbit! "Why would there be a rabbit this far down the beach?" she thought, and it did look a very *peculiar* sort of rabbit. It had long ears but it didn't have fur like a rabbit, more like seal skin. Molly looked up and down the sea, but all she could see were lots of bobbing heads. 'they must be afraid of me and won't come on the beach" she thought. Molly realised that the rabbit had a fishing hook in its paw... what was she going to do? It was too far to go and get help.

She decided to try and remove the hook - it didn't look too deep anyway, so she bent down, stroking the rabbit gently and told it not to be afraid. She carefully removed the hook without upsetting the rabbit too much. Molly took a hankie out of her pocket and held it tight against the paw. Soon it had stopped bleeding and Molly was pleased that the "rabbit" seemed to trust her. Max came over for a sniff, but decided that it wasn't anything really exciting and scampered off. The sea rabbit licked its paw, looked at Molly and blinked as if to say thank you then scurried back into the sea, popping his head up occasionally to see if Molly was still there.

After a while all the heads had disappeared beneath the sea and Molly called Max to head back up along the beach.

Max had found a plastic bottle and was dropping it down at Molly's feet so she could kick it, while he chased after it. He loved this game so much, barking and doing his little puppy dance while he waited for the bottle to be kicked. It did make Molly laugh out loud. Just as she was going to kick the bottle again Max started to run up the beach where they had just walked. She turned round to see why he had run off, only to see lots of the sea rabbits hopping towards her. They jumped over Max, dodging him as he chased after them, until they reached Molly. A big rabbit stood on its hind legs making him appear very regal and Molly was a little afraid, but he put out his paw and handed her what looked to be a stone. It was grey in colour but seemed to be glowing, Molly nervously took the stone, it was very cold to the touch.

The sea rabbit stood back and said

"I am Bogdown leader of the sea rabbits. You have done us a great service. Please hold the stone so that you may hear and talk to us."

Molly didn't know what to do, but tried to say without stuttering that she was called Molly and this was her dog Max. As her confidence began to seep back, she asked how the rabbit with the injured paw was feeling.

"Mudjar is a lot better thanks to you. It was a very kind deed" he replied whilst signalling for Mudjar to come forward. Molly crouched down and stroked Mudjar on the head.

"Hello Molly" he said, putting his uninjured paw out so she could shake it.

"How do you do" she laughed with surprise.

Max wasn't too sure about this and started to sniff Mudjar and he gave a little growl but Mudjar spoke in a soft strange language and Max's ears pricked up as he tilted his head to one side and Mudjar patted him on the head.

"What did you say to him?" asked Molly.

"I told him we were friends and we would do no harm" said Mudjar.

Max now seemed more interested in playing "catch the sea rabbits" but they leaped over him and ran far too quickly. He was soon out of breath and lay down next to Molly who was sitting cross legged on the sand. He still had one eye open just in case he missed anything interesting!

Bogdown and Mudjar sat next to Molly, as she asked all about their lives

"We are perhaps the last of the sea rabbits" said Bogdown "but we have a strong colony and we are left alone by the fishermen. Hundreds of years ago we sea rabbits could be seen all the time, as well as the clickers."

"Clickers?" asked Molly

"Yes the big fish-like creatures that click to talk."

"Oh I think you mean dolphins, they come up for air and are very friendly" Molly said.

"Yes that is correct, we see them very rarely now. It is a great shame. There have been a lot of changes. My grandfather told me of the ships with big wings"

Molly scratched head, what did he mean big wings?

"Ahhh" she said out loud "you mean sails!"

Bogdown continued

"and there have been great storms which have sunk many a ship. My grandfather rescued several of your kind. We used to go to the old wrecks when we were younger although our elders told us not to, as it was quite dangerous."

Molly would have loved to have stopped and listened to some more stories, but she was getting hungry and Granny would have her breakfast ready soon - and she had to feed Max too!

"I have to go I'm afraid" she said as she started to stand up "it has been a pleasure to meet you, and I hope I will see you again?"

"Of course" said Bogdown, "but remember to always bring the talking stone with you. We will look out for you and Max now we know you are our friends. Thank you for helping Mudjar"

"I was glad to help. Thank you for keeping me company." Said Molly

With that, all the sea rabbits hopped into the sea and disappeared beneath the waves.

2. A SURPRISE FOR MAX

Molly couldn't go down to the beach for several days as the weather was whipping up storm after storm. It would have been far too dangerous to walk on the beach as the waves were very high. She hoped all the sea rabbits would be safe and longed to see them again. Then some days later, when the weather was calmer and she knew the tide was out, she grabbed Max's lead and off she set. Molly had wrapped the talking stone in a nice clean hankie and had put it in the inside pocket of her coat for safe keeping. There was nobody on the beach which she was very pleased about, but she couldn't see any sea rabbits either.

Molly walked along feeling very downhearted. Max had found a plastic bottle and wanted her to kick it but she didn't want to play. Pulling up her scarf, with hands in pockets, she walked quickly to the end of the beach, looking out to sea, just in case she did see the sea rabbits.

She plonked herself down on the sea wall and Max jumped up beside her, knowing that she was feeling sad, and planted a big wet lick on the side of her face!

"Well" said Molly, putting her arm around him,

"I doubt you will be chasing any sea rabbits today."

He wasn't listening as he started to bark at a white object coming out of the sea. Goodness thought Molly what an earth is that? The white object was a small football! Mudjar was pushing it with his nose onto the beach. Molly quickly got the talking stone out and held it tight in her hand.

"The sea was so rough and this ball got lodged in some rocks near our home" he panted, "I thought Max would like to play with it"

Too right he did! He ran over and pushed the ball into the waves barking at Molly to hurry up and come and get it. She ran and quickly kicked the ball before the wave covered her shoes.

"Thank you Mudjar. I didn't think I would see you today." she said.

"We are very busy, we have some repairs to do" he replied

"Oh goodness your homes are safe aren't they?" she asked.

Max started barking,

"I'll kick the ball in a minute."

"Yes our homes are safe, we just have a lot of rocks that we need to clear as they're covering our seaweed patch. I must go now but we will see you soon."

And off he hopped into the sea.

"What do you think we can do to help Max?" she said.

Max just looked at her, pushed the ball with his nose to her feet and barked. Molly could see some of the seaweed covered in rocks, so she rolled up her jeans over her wellies, and began to move some of the lighter rocks out of the way. Max thought this was a game and kept dropping the ball with a splash next to her.

"At least" she thought " this will help the sea rabbits a little bit."

She picked up the ball and threw it really hard and Max bounded over to it. Molly walked out to sea, cleaned her hands on her jeans (what would Granny say about that?) and walked back up the beach, still playing football with Max. After the game Molly decided to leave the ball by the groyne. After all, the sea rabbits had very kindly loaned it to them and she didn't want to take it home - that would have been most impolite. Max wasn't the least bit impressed and showed his displeasure by refusing to go home. Molly had to go after him of course…

"Max you're very naughty at times" she said, bending down to put his lead on.

He looked up at her and gave her a great big sloppy lick on the hand and off they went.

3. A SECRET FROM THE SEA

The next day, although it was raining, Molly and Max walked quickly to the beach. The tide was changing now and was coming in, which meant Molly would have to be quick if she wanted to reach the end of the beach. Max went over to the groyne where they had left the ball yesterday and barked in delight as he found it.

"Good boy Max, but we will have to be quick today"

Max of course didn't care, as he chased the ball, pushing it with his nose so that it rolled into the sea.

"I'm wet enough all ready so *I'm* not getting it" Molly laughed.

Max's answer to that was to run up to her and have a good shake, spraying Molly with water, then he gave a loud bark and off again to chase the ball and pushed it to her feet.

Molly turned around as she heard her name being called. It was Mudjar,

"You are as wet as a sea rabbit" he laughed

"Yes You're right I am!" laughed Molly

As he stroked Max, he took Molly's hand and led her to a little cave that was hidden by part of the sea wall, half way down the beach. She had to get down on her knees to get into the cave but a least it was dry.

"You will be out of the rain in here and the tide will not reach so you are safe too."

Max on the other hand didn't know whether to play ball or chase the other sea rabbits who had hopped onto the beach, so he decided on both! Mudjar turned to Molly and thanked her for her help clearing some of the seaweed patch. The sea rabbits had also been very busy and life under the sea had returned back to normal after the storms.

"But we did find this" said Mudjar as he handed her what seemed to be a coin.

"We do not know what is, and thought we would ask for you to help."

Molly took the coin. It was very old and she had never seen one like it before. It was quite dirty so she gave it a gentle wipe with her handkerchief. On one side the words Georglvs III REX and a bust of a rather arrogant looking man. On the back it was less clear but she could see a harp and a date which looked like 1766. Mudjar asked what it was for and Molly began to explain that it was called money and would be used to buy things such as food or clothes. Mudjar looked very confused at this, so, she asked if it might have been from one of the ship wrecks. He thought for a moment and said that he had taken a look just after the storms and lots of things had been washed onto the sea bed from the wreck….although he shouldn't have been near there as Bogdown had forbidden it saying it was far too dangerous.

Molly promised not to tell and they both decided it would be a good idea to bury the coin in the cave, while Molly would investigate. Max was barking outside.

"I think he is telling me it's time to go home" she said

As she began to crawl outside she saw that indeed the tide was getting closer, so they said goodbye to Mudjar and the other sea rabbits that Max had been playing with and said they hoped to be out again tomorrow. Max knew, this time, to leave the ball at the groyne without a bark or a growl and off they trundled home.

4. THE NINE SURPRISES

Summer had arrived and the sun shone into Molly's bedroom waking her up very early. It was the school holidays but she decided to get up, as she didn't want anybody else to be on the beach. She quickly got dressed and told Max to be very quiet as they crept downstairs so she didn't wake anybody. Checking she had her magic stone, she grabbed the lead. Max was waiting by the door with his favourite ball in his mouth. Molly opened the door very quietly and off they set.

The tide was out and the beach was sandy, great fun for playing. Molly kicked the ball as hard as she could as Max scampered after it as fast as he could. She was getting quite good at kicking the ball now!

Molly saw Mudjar and a few other sea rabbits hop onto the beach.

"Hello" said Molly

"It's a beautiful day and Max is having so much fun."

He was trying to catch the sea rabbits again but without success.

"It is indeed a beautiful day" replied Mudjar. They carried on walking along the beach, talking about what they had both been doing since they had last seen each other. Molly looked out to sea and as she did she saw lots of fishes jumping….and then to her amazement she saw a school of dolphins.

"Goodness Mudjar can you see that? There are so many dolphins, there are at least 7 no there are 9!" Molly exclaimed.

"Ah the clickers, you are indeed very fortunate to see so many. They"re feeding on the fish" he replied.

Molly knew they were dolphins and not porpoises because she had read that the fin of a porpoise was more triangular, and their snouts were a lot shorter. Her Mummy and Daddy with Granny had taken her once to see Fungie the Dolphin, in Dingle Bay a few summers back. They had boarded the boat and as the boat left the harbour, all of a sudden a grey flash appeared out of the water and then dived under a wave. Fungie followed the boat for a while playing a game of now you see me, now you don't, as he dived into the water and then would reappear.

The boat stopped and everybody peered over the sides and it seemed ages before Fungie popped his head up, gave several clinks and swam over to Granny and nudged her hand! Molly cried in delight - it was one of the best sights she had ever seen….and now, today, on the beach 9 dolphins had appeared. She so wanted to tell Granny what an amazing sight she had seen, but Molly was afraid that lots of grown-ups would come down to the beach to look for the dolphins and that would scare the sea rabbits. Mudjar sensed that Molly was feeling sad and said

'Molly are you not happy to see the clickers?"

"Oh I am very happy" she replied.

"But I would like to tell my Granny, but if I do I think lots of people will come down to the beach and then I won't see you and that will make me very sad."

Max gave a bark as if to say and I would be sad too!

"Do not worry" said Mudjar, "we do get a lot of your kind on the beach when the clickers feed. We are very careful that they do not see us. The sea will be coming in very close to the land for a while so they will not be able to get all the way down."

Molly noticed the sea was getting closer and Mudjar told her it would be best for her to go home.

"We will see you very soon" he said.

"Come on Max it's time to go" Molly said.

She looked out to sea and saw that the dolphins were now swimming off into the distance.

"It looks like they've had their breakfast Max, I think it's time for ours" she said.

Molly waved bye to Mudjar and the other sea rabbits and then they headed home, very hungry!

5. THE BIRTHDAY PARTY

It was soon to be Molly's friend's birthday. His name was James and he was slightly younger that Molly. She had chosen a present for James that she knew he would love and now all she had to do was wait for tomorrow as there was going to be a birthday party. She was looking forward to this very much!

Max was barking impatiently by the door. He wanted to go and chase the sea rabbits.

"Oh Max do be quiet and behave, you will wake everybody up!" Molly said, as she headed to the door.

She noticed a note pinned to the notice board just as she was about to leave, which said

'Molly, we are very sorry but James isn't very well and the party has been cancelled."

"Oh dear poor James," she thought, "he will be so disappointed."

Molly walked along the beach thinking about how sad James would be that his birthday party had been cancelled. She wondered how she could cheer him up. Just then Mudjar came hopping up.

"Hello Molly" he said, "You look quite sad, whatever is the matter?"

"It's my friend's birthday and he was going to have a party but he's not very well" she replied.

Mudjar cocked his head to one side,

"What is a birth..day?" he asked.

"It's the day you were born, and we sometimes have a party, this means that lots of your friends come to your house, you have lots of yummy food and we play games. You know how Max likes to chase the other rabbits, and they hop and run? well that's a game."

Molly said. "It's just a special happy day, but James is poorly so there will be no party."

'Molly could you wait here for a little while? I think I might be able to help"

And with that he hopped into the sea and disappeared under a wave. She sat on a rock and watched Max and the other sea rabbits playing their game, but Max was getting tired and he lay on the sand panting for a while….then barking as if to say "I've had a rest, now we can play again!"

After a while Mudjar surfaced then hopped to where she was sitting. He had in his hand something that looked like seaweed.

'This is from the clickers, you will need to put this just here, as he pointed to her forehead "and it will take away the badness that is making James ill, but do not keep it on for very long as it has very strong powers."

"Oh thank you Mudjar" Molly said "I will go and see James as soon as I have taken Max home, and please thank the clickers it is most kind."

"It is best if you do this as soon as possible" he said "we will come down a little way with you, as Max seems to be enjoying this game."

Molly fed Max when they got home, then as quickly as she could she went to see James. When Molly arrived he was asleep in his bed. She took the seaweed out of her pocket. It was still a little wet, but she placed it on his forehead as Mudjar had instructed and thought that 5 minutes would be long enough. Taking the seaweed off his head she put it back into her pocket and went to sit in the chair and see if James would wake up. After a while he began to stir,

"Oh hello Molly, I've had a very strange dream, I was swimming with dolphins and seals and we were all playing. I must say I feel a lot better and I'm very hungry" James said.

Molly went downstairs to tell James's mummy that he was awake and feeling hungry.

"That is a good sign, he hasn't eaten anything since yesterday and I was getting a bit worried" said James's mummy "I will take him a sandwich and a bit of jelly and ice cream, would you like some too Molly?"

'That would be lovely, thank you so much."

Molly did like jelly and ice cream it was one of her favourite things to eat.

Later on James's mummy came up to see how James was feeling.

'My goodness James you seem to have got better, how are you feeling?"

'Much better mummy and I think I will be well enough for my party" he laughed.

"Well let's wait and see how you are in the morning and if you do feel better we can ring everybody to say the party is still on."

"OK mummy but I really really do feel loads better" James protested.

Molly went back home and told Max the good news when they were sitting on her bed. Max's head was tilting from side to side as she told him what had happened, she knew he understood what she was saying, as he was such a clever dog.

The next day the phone call came and the party was to go ahead. Molly was so excited, but she also knew that tomorrow she should thank Mudjar and the clickers again. The seaweed did indeed have magic powers.

The party was a great success with lots of yummy food and great games.

6. A NEW GAME FOR MAX

Max got the ball from the groyne and carried it down to the sandy bit of the beach. Molly kicked it hard and it bounced across some stones causing it to go the opposite way to the direction that Max was running. Molly laughed and told Max he was a clever boy as he jumped up and caught it anyway.

A few of the Sea rabbits were basking in the early morning sun near to the wall at the bottom of the beach. Molly already had the talking stone in her hand and looked out to see if she could see Mudjar or Bogdown. Max went racing ahead, ball in mouth and played chase. Mudjar was just coming out of the sea, as Molly reached the wall.

"Hello" she said as Mudjar hopped up to her and put his paw out

"Hello Molly, my paw is better now because you helped me, and the hole has gone!" he said.

Molly looked to where the fishing hook had been and indeed it had healed!

"That *is* good, I am very pleased" said Molly.

Max was barking and running into the sea. Molly and Mudjar turned to look to see what was happening. A new game had been invented! Max would push the ball into the sea and the sea rabbits would take it and swim a little way down the beach. Max didn't know where the ball had gone, until the sea rabbits pushed it onto the sand. Max ran down, got the ball and pushed it into the sea again and the whole game began again.

Molly laughed and said "Well, Max seems to be enjoying himself"

"Yes indeed" Mudjar replied.

All of a sudden Bogdown appeared and began to talk to Mudjar in their strange language. Molly knew it was quite serious by the look on Bogdown's face. They talked for a long time, before Mudjar turned to Molly and said:

"We are very sorry but we must go - we have heard from the clickers that some of our kind are in trouble."

"Oh dear" said Molly "is there anything I can do to help?"

"No thank you Molly it is very kind of you, but we must prepare."

Molly was just about to call Max but Bogdown said

"Let Max play he is enjoying himself, why don't you go and play too"

So Molly ran to where Max was playing and began to join in the game of hunt the ball. There was a lot of laughing from Molly and Max barked in delight as she played. The Sea rabbits made a "chatting" sound too when they put the ball on the beach. But you just never knew where the ball would be…so Max was getting tired and rested for a while. "I think it's time to go home now Max" Molly said.

The sea rabbits gave the ball to Max and off they strolled down he beach, turning to wave goodbye to the sea rabbits.

7. LOTTIE

The sun was just rising and Molly knew it was going to be another beautiful day.

As she quickly got dressed, Max was sitting on her bed and making his funny little noise when he knew it was time to go out for his walk.

"Sshhh…" said Molly "We don't want to wake anybody or they might want to come and walk with us" she whispered.

Max tilted his head and stood by the door without a sound. It was indeed going to be a lovely day and because it was still early it was still a little cool so Molly put on her jumper over her tee-shirt and tied up her boots, making sure she had the talking stone with her.

They both crept out of the house, with Max nudging at her leg as if to tell her to be quiet.

The tide was midway on the beach but Molly knew it was going out, as she always checked to make sure. She didn't want to get stranded on the beach!. Max had run ahead and was playing in the waves and getting very wet! Molly could see at the end of the beach that there were a few sea rabbits basking in the sun. Bogdown and Mudjar came hopping down and as they did Molly took out the magic stone

"Good morning Bogdown and Mudjar, it's a beautiful day isn't it?" said Molly.

"It is indeed" they replied.

"Come Molly I have somebody I wish you to meet." said Bogdown as he pointed with his paw to the end of the beach. Molly was most intrigued and called over to Max for him to follow. When they reached the group of sea rabbits, Bogdown called out and all of a sudden a sea rabbit appeared from by the rocks and came hopping over to Molly and Max.

"Hello, I am Lottie, she said shyly."

She was a very pretty rabbit with big brown eyes, her fur was dappled a grey and silver colour, but the silver shone brightly when the sun caught it.

"Hello Lottie it's very nice to meet you" Molly replied. 'This is Max my dog and he's being very naughty!"

"He is very wet" said Lottie.

"Yes he is" laughed Molly "he likes to play in the sea"

"Can he swim like me?" asked Lottie.

"I'm afraid not, he only goes a little way in".

Max looked at Molly as if to say, "I can swim thank you. I just choose not to most of the time!", before wandering off for his game of chase. Molly wanted to ask why Lottie had different colouring than all the other sea rabbits but Bogdown interrupted her thoughts.

"Lottie is from a far away sea and the clickers helped her to escape from the big boats that take the fish. There were only a few left in her colony and they are very lucky to escape. Some of them are very sick, injured and exhausted from the journey, but we have plenty of the seaweed with healing powers." He said."

Oh is there anything I can do to help?" answered Molly.

'Thank you Molly that is most kind. There is a flower I need, but it is a little too high for any of us to gather….. maybe you could pick it for me if I show you which one?" Bogdown asked before hopping over to the bank where the flowers were on a bush. It was a little way up and Molly had to scrabble over rocks before reaching the grassy area. Max cocked his head to one side before giving a bark and running over to where Molly was climbing. It wasn't very steep. Molly knew Granny would not want her to do anything dangerous. She reached up and collected some of the flowers which she put in her hankie, before making her way back down.

'Thank you Molly you have been most helpful" Bogdown said as she handed him the flowers, "we can now make a stronger potion for the weaker ones. I'm afraid we must leave as time is very important."

Molly was a little sad but understood that they must go, as the sea rabbits hopped into the sea. She called Max and they heading back down the beach but Lottie appeared to say thank you to Molly and gave Max a pat, and he returned a big wet lick to Lottie's face. She laughed and saying goodbye as she returned to the sea.

8. TWO LOST DUCKINGS

Max was barking at something near to the end of the beach, as Molly ran up to where he was waiting for her.

'Stop now Max" she said as she came to the clump of rocks near the small cave. To her surprise there were two little ducklings huddled against each other. Max stopped barking and began to sniff one of the ducks...

"Quack quack quack!" it said angrily.

Molly laughed and said 'See, he is telling you off! Poor things they look cold. I think we had better see if Mudjar or Bogdown is around, they will know what to do."

They started to walk down to the end of the beach, but Mudjar was already hopping towards them with Bogdown following behind him.

"Hello Molly," he said and patted Max on the head

"Hello Mudjar, I'm glad we found you, there are two little ducklings by the rocks and I think they may be lost"

"Oh that is good news Molly, their mother and father have been looking for them. Please show me where they are."

Molly took Mudjar to where they were huddled. "Quack quack quack!" said the one who had told Max off earlier. Mudjar spoke in a strange tone and the duckling lowered its head, he carried on in the strange tone and the ducklings replied. Mudjar called for Bogdown then spoke to him in sea rabbit, before Bogdown scurried off into the sea.

"I have asked him to go and get the parents. The little ducklings didn't come home last night and they are very worried."

After a while Molly could hear the flapping of wings. It was Mummy and Daddy duck. They made a perfect landing very close to the beach and waddled over until they saw Molly and Max. Mudjar spoke to them and told them it was safe so they moved closer to Molly. Mudjar explained to Molly, that Mummy duck had taken the ducklings to practise their swimming because it was nice and calm but the two ducklings had gone off around the cove. The chugging of the boat had been a warning and Mummy duck quacked to all the ducklings that it was time to go and off they flew leaving these two ducklings behind! When the ducklings returned back to the cove they saw that they were all alone and as their legs were getting tired they waddled up the beach.

"What shall we do?" asked one of the ducklings. 'mummy will come back for us in a while" replied the other duckling.

But as they waited and waited, the tide and the sea mist began to creep in, and the two ducklings were getting cold and frightened. They waddled up the beach a little more until they saw an opening to a small cave.

"We had better wait in here it will be a little warmer if we huddle up" and that's just what they did.

Max you are a clever boy for finding the ducklings said Molly and they all agreed. The ducklings gave Mummy and Daddy duck great big hugs and before they flew back home, they promised to come back and visit Molly and Max very soon.

Bogdown said "if you keep this up Max, we will have to make you on honorary sea rabbit!"

…..But that is a story for another day.

9. SEA RABBIT TREASURE

It was just starting to rain when Molly took Max to the beach.

"I hope it doesn't get too rainy, or we will have to be quick Max" she said.

Max tilted his head to one side and gave a bark, which Molly thought was more of an "Oh no we won't, I have sea rabbits to chase", sort of bark.

Max found the ball at the groyne, picked it up and ran down the beach to find some sea rabbits to play with. Molly called out for him to come back as it had begun to rain really hard. It would be better if they went home. Then Molly remembered the small cave, where the ducklings had sheltered, so she ran as quickly as she could. Just as she was about to go into the cave, Bogdown hopped over to her.

"It is not a very good day for you to be walking" he said.

"No it isn't" she replied, "but Max doesn't mind what weather it is". "I think we had better just go into the cave and wait for the rain to pass."

A few of the other sea rabbits had joined them in the cave, and Max came in with his ball, then dropped it on the ground when he saw Lottie, and he trotted over to her and waited for her to pat him on the head.

"Good boy" said Lottie.

"Woof" said Max.

As the rain got stronger and the sky began to get darker Molly remembered she had a torch in her pocket. At least it wouldn't be so gloomy. She put the torch on and had a good look around the cave. Although it was small there was lots space if you were little enough. As she moved the light around something caught her eye, something that was shining.

"Bogdown" she asked what do you think that is over there?"

"I do not know Molly, let me go and see. Could you shine your bright glow, so I can take a look?"

Molly knew he meant the torch, so she shone it to where Bogdown was hopping to.

"Molly" he said 'there are astonishing colours, let me bring these to you."

And indeed there were - small smooth pebbles of reds, greens and blues. Lottie hopped over to join them. She looked a little scared, as she stared from Molly to Bogdown.

"You have found my treasure" she said.

"I have found these in the sea and on the beach, so I have hidden them in the cave. I do not want anybody to steal them. They must be very precious."

Molly picked one up and took a close look, then she realised that it was glass that had been washed with sand in the sea. It had made the pebbles smooth and a little dull, but still very beautiful.

"These are very precious and I think they should be called sea rabbit treasure" Molly said.

She knew that Lottie would be very sad if she knew it was just glass, and she didn't want to hurt her feelings.

"I think it is a very good idea to keep it safe in the cave."

All the sea rabbits agreed it was much safer and they would help Lottie find some more.

'Molly I think it would be best if you went now, as the rain is getting stronger" Bogdown whispered to Molly.

"Yes I think you are right, Granny will be worrying. Come Max we must go home. Bring the ball."

Max didn't really want to go home. It was much drier in the cave, but he knew there would be food when he got home. He gave

Lottie a lick and off they went. Max left the ball at the groyne, but it rolled down toward the sea. Molly went to pick it up and as she did, there was a small blue glass pebble! She put it in her pocket, thinking that Lottie would be very pleased with that. The ball was placed so it wouldn't roll away, then Max and Molly headed home as quickly as they could.

By the time they got home, Granny had made hot chocolate and lots of hot buttered crumpets. Then Molly washed Max and had a nice warm bath, then snuggled down by the roaring fire.

10. THE CLICKERS

Molly had been talking to Bogdown while Max was chasing some of the sea rabbits, who were having a fun time jumping over him and running away. Bogdown told Molly that he would be gone for a little while, as he had a surprise for them. He raised his eyebrows, flopped his ears and winked at Molly then hopped into the sea and began to swim off around the cove.

Molly thought Bogdown was being very mysterious, then noticed something in the sea. She realised it was a dolphin, and then another and then quite a few more. They began to swim towards her and as they did, they jumped out of the sea and over each other before coming as close as they dared. One of the dolphins stuck his head out of the sea and began to make that lovely clicking noise that only dolphins and porpoises seem to make, before the other dolphins joined in. Molly jumped for joy at the amazing sight and sound, before seeing that Bogdown was standing next to her

"Molly" he said 'the clickers are saying that it is a pleasure to see a friend of the sea rabbits and they know you will do no harm."

Molly was so amazed, and said that this was the best thing she had ever seen in her whole life.

"Please tell the clickers that it is also a pleasure to meet them, they are all so beautiful and very clever with their swimming."

Max, who had heard the clicking but had been too busy playing ball with the other sea rabbits came to the water's edge and began to very carefully take a few steps into the water. He sniffed the air and went in a little further then dropped the ball into the sea and pushed it towards one of the clickers. The clicker dived into the water and came up just where the ball was, and flicked it over to where Max was waiting. Max was delighted and he began to swim with the ball again and pushed it towards the clicker. The clicker did it again!

"Woof!" said Max as he looked at Molly and Bogdown.

"I think he has a new game and he's being very brave" Molly laughed.

Max was soon playing ball with the clickers and the sea rabbits and was having the best time. The clicker said something to Bogdown, then turned to the other clickers.

'They must go now Molly" said Bogdown.

Molly called Max out of the sea, but he was so enjoying himself he didn't want to leave. The clickers did one final jump in the sea, gave a wave with their tails, then dived back into sea all at the same time. Max push the ball out hoping for the best, but it just bobbed on the waves, until Lottie went to rescue it and pushed it back to the beach. Max stood by Molly and shook himself, spraying water all over her.

"HEY!" said Molly laughing

"I don't think he's very happy" she said to Bogdown

"I think you are right, Molly!" he replied.

"Come on Max we really do have to get home now, I'm sure the dolphins will come back and play with you again another day."

With that he gave a wag and trotted off down the beach towards home, perfectly happy again.

'Thank you Bogdown you are so kind to get the clickers to visit and I will never forget seeing them".

"You are welcome" Bogdown replied then hopped into the sea to join the other sea rabbits.

"Come back and see us soon Molly" Bogdown shouted as he disappeared below the waves.

11. A NEW FRIEND FOR MAX

Another beautiful day began to break, as Molly and Max strolled down to the bottom of the beach. Max raced ahead as he could see the Sea rabbits begin to appear. He woofed his greeting to Lottie as she hopped up to him and stroked his head.

"Hello Max, Hello Molly" she said 'my friends are a lot better now and they have come to say thank you."

There were lots of new sea rabbits and they hopped over shyly at first but Lottie told them that Molly and Max were friends. Max lifted his head and began to sniff as they came closer. There, by the big rocks and the sea, was a very small sea rabbit which seemed to be a little afraid. Max took a few steps forward, but the sea rabbit hopped around to one of the rocks to hide.

"Is she still growing, she's very small compared to the other sea rabbits?" asked Molly.

Lottie told Molly that the sea rabbit was called Agnes. She had got one of her front paws caught in a fishing net, and she had lost part of her paw. She had been very ill when she was younger because of her accident and that is why she was still very little. Max crept round the rock and Agnes hopped quickly and hid behind Lottie.

"I think she is a little afraid of Max, but give her time I think they will become great friends" Lottie said.

Molly told Max to go play chase with the other sea rabbits, before sitting down on the beach with Lottie to watch all the running and hopping. Agnes still kept her distance from Molly and stood very close to the rock she had been hiding behind. After a while Max was tired out after all the chasing and came to lie down at Molly's feet. Then a very strange thing happened. As Max was lying down Agnes came over and snuggled up very close to him. He opened his eyes, raised his head and gave Agnes a big lick on the head. Agnes snuggled in even closer, and they both fell asleep.

"Well Molly, I did tell you they would become great friends. Agnes is still very scared and doesn't play too much with the other sea rabbits, so this is indeed a good step for her" Lottie said.

Molly was without a doubt surprised to see the two of them all cuddled up and really didn't want to tell Max it was time to go home, but they had to go as it was nearly time for breakfast. Lottie woke Agnes and began to speak to her, and Molly gently called Max, but Max sat down instead and looked straight at Agnes, then gave a little woof.

"I think he's saying goodbye" Molly said,

but Agnes hopped over and onto Max's back! Max stood up and walked very carefully down the beach while Agnes clung tightly.

"Well I never" said Molly "he has never let any of the sea rabbits do that before."

After a little way down the beach Agnes whispered something into Max's ear and he stopped, and sat down. She slid down his back and hopped to face him, then planted a big kiss on his nose, before hopping off to Lottie. Molly went over to Max, turned to the sea rabbits and waved bye bye before heading home.

"Well Max you have made a little sea rabbit very happy" Molly laughed.

"Woof woof" came the reply

….and Max, in typical 'max" fashion (as he isn't very good at paying attention) thought "now where is that ball I saw earlier…..I think it's time for a game!"

12. GRANNY

Molly and Max were just getting ready to go down to the beach, when Molly realised she didn't have her talking stone in her hankie. Molly looked high and low in her room but she still couldn't find it.

"Good Morning Molly" said Granny as they came into the kitchen.

"Good morning Granny, you are up very early" she replied as she gave Granny a great big hug.

"You look a little worried Molly, whatever is the matter?"

"Erm well…."

Molly didn't want to ask Granny if she had seen the stone.

"Have you seen my blue flowered hankie?"

"Ah yes Molly I took it out of your jeans when I washed them. It's just over here. Oh and I found this inside too..." said Granny as she held out the stone. Molly was nervous because she didn't want to explain why she had a stone in her hankie, as it was rather a very strange thing to do!

"Can you just wait a while before you go out, I want to show you something?" Granny asked, before going into her room.

Granny came back with a hankie and there, wrapped inside, guess what Molly saw? A stone just like Molly's!

"When I was a little girl" Granny began "I used to go to the beach almost every day - and one day I saw a sea rabbit! We became good friends and I had lots of adventures with them."

"Oh Granny I am so pleased you know about the sea rabbits! Will you come down to the beach with us to see them?"

"What a lovely idea – but you will have to walk a little slower Molly, as I'm not as young as you - and we had better not forget our talking stones!" Granny laughed.

Max of course ran ahead and was getting impatient as Molly and Granny were walking slowly down to the beach.

'Max you will just have to wait! Here, get the ball, good boy" she said.

He ran to pick the ball up then ran back to Molly and dropped it at her feet.

"I have to kick it now to him. He loves this game" Molly explained to Granny,

When they got to the bottom of the beach, none of the sea r rabbits were there.

"I hope I'm not scaring them" said Granny,

"No I'm sure they will be here soon!" Molly replied.

And sure enough a little head popped out of the sea, ducked down again, then the ripples on the sea, showed that one of the sea rabbits was heading to the beach. Mudjar hopped onto the beach saw Molly then stopped. Molly walked over with Max.

"Hello Mudjar, it's very nice to see you. That is my Granny over there and when she was a little girl she used to come down to the beach. She has a talking stone too and remembers the sea rabbits from long ago!"

Mudjar hopped over towards Granny.

"I am Mudjar it is very nice to meet you" he said as he put his paw out. Granny took his paw and gave it a little shake.

"It is very nice to meet you too!" she said.

Bogdown hopped up to join them and Mudjar spoke to him in their strange language.

"Ah" said Bogdown " you also have a talking stone! can you remember who gave it to you?" he asked.

Granny thought about that for a little while then replied

"It was a sea rabbit of silver fur with dark stripes and he was called Jimjam."

"Jimjam, yes he had many adventures and travelled to many places. He still lives nearby, maybe Mudjar would go and see if he will come to the beach. What name do you go by?" said Bogdown.

"My name is Rosie, but it was a very long time ago. He might not remember me" Granny replied.

Bogdown said something to Mudjar and off he went into the sea.

After a while Mudjar came hopping onto the beach with another much older sea rabbit, that Molly had never seen before. Granny walked down to the sea edge,

"Hello Jimjam, it has been a very long time!" she said.

"Yes it has Rosie, but it is a great pleasure to see you again. You have changed from the girl I remember who was always running and playing with the sea rabbits, but I have also changed and I'm not so fast these days" he laughed.

Jimjam and Granny sat on the rocks talking, while Molly, Bogdown, Mudjar and Max went off to play.

The tide was coming in and Molly went over to Granny.

"I suppose we have to go home soon?" she said

"Yes Molly I just want to say goodbye to Jimjam," Granny replied

After a while all the goodbyes were said and Jimjam even gave Rosie a little hug! Granny turned to Molly

"I will tell you of all the adventures I had when I was a little girl. Jimjam was the leader of the sea rabbits then. He was very wise, but he also played lots of tricks too!" she laughed.

"Oh tell me now" said Molly

"I'm tired and we need to get home, I will have a cup of tea then I will tell you."

Molly gave Granny a great big hug, held her hand as they carried on walking towards home and said

"I'm glad we both know about the sea rabbits"

Jimjam chuckled as they walked away and called after them

"come and see us again soon, and I will tell you all the mischief Rosie and I got up to…"

but those are stories for another day!

Further adventures of The Sea Rabbits will soon be available at www.thesearabbits.com **and on Amazon.**

ABOUT THE AUTHOR

Pip Carr lives mostly in the beautiful garden county of Wicklow in Ireland with her husband and dog, She has a grown up son in Canada. Whilst she is an accomplished writer, this is her first foray into the world of children's fiction.

Printed in Great Britain
by Amazon